Contents

Hansel and Gretel

Once upon a time a poor woodcutter and his second wife lived on the edge of a forest. Hansel and Gretel, the woodcutter's children by his first wife, lived with them. They were very poor indeed and there came a day when they had no more food and no more money to buy any more food.

"Whatever are we to do, husband?" said the wife. "We cannot feed our children and we are all going to starve."

HANSEL
AND GRETEL
and other stories

Retold by
MARY HOFFMAN

Illustrated by
ANNA CURREY

MACMILLAN

First published in 2000 in *The Macmillan Treasury of Nursery Stories*.
This collection published in 2002 by Macmillan Children's Books
A division of Macmillan Publishers Limited
25 Eccleston Place, London SW1W 9NF,
Basingstoke and Oxford
Associated companies throughout the world.
www.macmillan.com

ISBN 0 333 96138 2

1 3 5 7 9 8 6 4 2

Printed in Hong Kong

"I don't know," replied the wretched man. "I suppose we must keep on cutting wood and hope that things will get better."

"That's no good," said the wife. "We need a plan. I think we should take the children out into the forest with us, give them a last slice of bread each and then contrive to leave them, so that they are lost."

"But they will be devoured by wild beasts!" the woodcutter protested.

"Better that than for us to have to watch them starve. It will be a quicker death," said his wife.

And in the end, reluctantly, the woodcutter agreed with her. Now Hansel, who was a light sleeper, had heard all this conversation and went to tell his sister. She was horrified. "What can we do?" she cried.

"Don't worry, sister," said Hansel. "They may have a plan, but so do I."

And he went out into the moonlight and picked up handfuls of white pebbles from outside their hut.

In the morning, the whole family set off for the forest but, as they walked, Hansel kept stopping to leave a trail

of white pebbles so that he and Gretel could find their way back. When his stepmother noticed that he was not keeping up, she asked what he was doing and he replied, "I'm looking back because I can see my little white cat sitting on the roof as if to say goodbye to me."

"Foolish boy!" said his stepmother. "That is not your little white cat. It is the sunlight shining on the roof tiles."

The parents left their children, with a slice of bread each and a warm fire, in a glade in the forest, while they worked at cutting trees. But the woodcutter had fixed up a broken branch so that it knocked against a withered tree in the wind and sounded like his axe. By the time the children had discovered the trick, their parents were long gone.

But they ate their bread and waited till nightfall, when

the moon came out. Then they followed the trail of white pebbles back to their home. When they knocked at the door, their stepmother scolded them for getting lost, but their father was very pleased to see them.

And it happened that the food shortage eased and so the father was very glad that the plan to lose them in the forest had not succeeded. Time passed and there was another famine in the land. Again the woodcutter's family was reduced to their last half-loaf of bread and with no prospect of any more food.

So the woodcutter's wife suggested the same idea again. "Only this time we must take them further into the forest so that they cannot find their way back. This is the only way to save ourselves."

Secretly the woodcutter thought it would be better to share their last mouthfuls of food with their children and all starve together. But since he had said yes the time before, he didn't know how to say no this time, so in the end he agreed. But the children had overheard their parents talking and knew what was going to happen. Only this time the door was locked and Hansel could not collect any pebbles. "Don't worry," he told his sister. "I shall think of something."

In the morning, the parents gave each child a slice of bread, but Hansel crumbled his in his pocket and dropped the crumbs behind him as they walked. "What are you doing?" asked his stepmother sharply.

"I am looking at my little white pigeon on the roof that looks as if it is saying goodbye to me," said Hansel.

"Nonsense!" said his stepmother. "That is no pigeon. It is the morning sunlight shining on the chimney."

The parents took their children deeper into the forest than before and built them a fire. Then they went away to work, telling the children they would be back before dark. Of course, they never returned. At midday, Gretel shared her piece of bread with Hansel. And when it got dark and the moon came up, they tried to find their way home, but birds had come and eaten up all Hansel's crumbs, so they had no trail to follow.

"Now we are truly lost," wept Gretel.

"No, no," said Hansel, trying to keep her spirits up. "We'll soon find the way."

But they didn't. They walked all that night and all the next day, lying down to sleep in the leaves when they were tired, but they were still no nearer to finding their home.

By now they were very hungry, for there was nothing but a few berries to eat in the forest. They were lucky that they hadn't come across any wild beasts, because they would have been tasty morsels for a hungry bear or wolf.

Tired and hungry, they eventually stumbled into a clearing where there was a cosy little house. And when they got nearer to it, they could see that it was all made of food!

The roof was made of gingerbread, the windows of spun sugar and the door and window sills of lovely sweet cake.

It was a long time since Hansel and Gretel had tasted anything sweet and they were very hungry, so they couldn't resist. Hansel reached up and broke off a piece of gingerbread roof. And Gretel, I'm sorry to say, began to lick one of the windows. How delicious it tasted!

But then the cottage door flew open and a very old woman came hobbling out on two sticks. The children were terrified but she seemed kindly enough.

"What charming children!" she said. "Who brought you here?"

Hansel and Gretel explained how they were lost in the forest and the old woman invited them in and gave them apple pancakes and glasses of milk. She didn't say anything about finding them eating her house.

When their stomachs were full, the children became very sleepy and the old woman showed them to two little white beds. Hansel and Gretel thought themselves in heaven as they fell asleep.

But they were wrong. The old woman wasn't really sweet and kind. She was really a witch! She had it in mind to eat the two children and, in fact, her house was made of sweet goodies especially to entice children to her. She was a very wicked witch indeed.

In the morning, before the children were awake, she seized Hansel and locked him in a cage, because he was the plumper of the two. Then she shook Gretel awake and told her she must do all the housework and cook nice food for her brother, who was to be fattened up to be eaten.

Gretel was horrified, but she had to do what the witch told her. Now Hansel was fed chicken stew and sausages and gravy and dumplings and spotted dick with custard, while Gretel got only dry crackers and cheese rinds. Every day the witch reached into the cage to feel Hansel's finger, but her eyesight was so bad that he was able to deceive her by thrusting a chicken bone out.

"Why does he never get any fatter?" grumbled the witch, as she felt the bone.

But after four weeks she was too impatient to wait any more.

"Boil up water on the stove," she told Gretel. "I'm going to cook that boy today."

Gretel wept and wailed but it was no good. She had to heat up the water.

"I'm going to bake some bread to have with him," said the witch. "I've made the dough. Now just creep into the oven for me and tell me if it's hot enough."

Now the wicked witch meant to shut the oven door on Gretel and bake her! But Gretel had her suspicions so

she asked the witch, "What exactly do you mean? Would you mind showing me yourself?"

"Stupid girl!" muttered the witch. But she clambered into the oven and BANG! Gretel shut the door on her. And the wicked witch was burned to a cinder.

Gretel rushed to get her keys from the rack and released Hansel from his cage. They embraced each other heartily, crying with relief over their escape from the witch.

Now they had nothing to fear so they explored the house and found chests of pearls and other precious jewels. Hansel stuffed his pockets with them, saying, "These are better than pebbles!" Gretel filled the pockets of her pinafore. She also helped herself to a nice piece of pie and a couple of apples but Hansel felt so full that he wasn't interested in food.

Their next thought was to get home, but they had no idea where they were. They started off in what they thought was the right direction. Before long they came to a broad stretch of water with no bridge in sight. But there was a white duck swimming on the water and Gretel asked her if she would take them across.

When they were both across, they walked a bit further and after a while their surroundings began to seem familiar. Then with joy they recognised the path to their old home. They rushed in through the door and found their father sitting very lonely in the downstairs room.

Their stepmother had died while they had been away and their father had missed his children terribly. He was so glad to see them again. And he was amazed when he saw all the pearls and jewels. From that day onwards they always had enough to eat. But Hansel never touched gingerbread again.

Rumpelstiltskin

O nce upon a time there was a poor miller who found himself called to do business with a king. You might have thought that would be enough for him, but no, he had to start boasting, so that the king would think he was someone important.

"I have a daughter," he said, which was true enough. "And she is remarkably beautiful," he said, which was also true. But then he added, "And she has this gift, that she can spin straw into gold."

Oh, foolish miller! Why didn't he stop after saying he had a beautiful daughter? For no one can spin straw into gold and he was just asking for trouble.

"Really?" said the king, raising his eyebrows and looking at the miller's dusty apron. "That is a very useful gift indeed. Bring her to me so that she may show off this skill."

Now the miller was well and truly in the soup. He wished he had kept his mouth shut, but it was too late for that. He had to bring his daughter to the palace. The king showed her into a large room full of straw, with a spinning-wheel in the middle.

"Here you are, my dear," he said, kindly. "As much straw as you like. Turn it all into gold by morning or you must die."

The poor girl didn't know what to do. She hadn't the faintest idea how to start turning straw into gold, any more than you or I do. So she sat on a bale of straw and wept.

Suddenly a funny little man appeared and asked her what was the matter.

"I have to turn all this straw into gold by morning," sobbed the girl, "or I shall die."

"Well, that's nothing to cry about," said the little man. "I can do that. But what will you give me if I do?"

The miller's daughter said she would give him her necklace and the little man agreed. The girl curled up on the straw and slept peacefully all night to the hum of the spinning-wheel, until the little man needed the bale she was lying on, because he had filled every reel with spun gold.

By dawn the little man had disappeared and the room was full of reels of gold. The king couldn't believe his eyes and the miller's daughter was mightily relieved. But, that evening, the king took her to an even bigger room with even more straw in it and gave her a spinning-wheel.

"You did so well yesterday," he said, smiling. "I'm sure you will manage to turn this lot of straw into gold too."

The girl wasn't sure at all, until the little man appeared again. He looked at all the straw.

"What will you give me this time?" he asked.

"The ring from my finger," said the girl, taking it off. And, though it was of no great value, the little man took it and set to work. By morning the room was full of spun gold.

And was the king content? You can probably guess by now what he did. He took the miller's daughter into a barn, filled with straw from floor to ceiling, so that there was scarcely room for the spinning-wheel to be squeezed in.

"This is the last time I shall ask you, my dear," said the king. "But if you turn all this straw into gold, I shall make you my queen." (For the miller's daughter really was very pretty.) "But," added the king, "if you do not, I'm afraid the terms are as before and you will die."

The girl sat at the spinning-wheel and wept. It didn't even cheer her up to see the little man appear, for she knew she had nothing left to give him.

"What, nothing?" he asked, when she explained the situation.

"Nothing at all," she said.

"All right," said the little man. "I will do it for you, but you must promise me that, if you ever become queen, you will give me your first-born child."

So the girl promised; what else could she do? And by morning the whole barn was filled with spun gold. The king clasped her in his arms and kissed her and she was queen within a week.

It had all happened so suddenly that it seemed like a dream and she forgot all about her promise. A year after the marriage, the young queen gave birth to a healthy baby boy. She was delighted with him, like any new mother. But while she was cooing over her pretty baby, the funny little man suddenly appeared in the royal bedroom and reminded her of her promise.

She was horrified. "You can't mean it!" she cried,

clutching her precious baby son. "I shall never give him up. Think of something else."

And she offered him all the riches of her husband's kingdom— jewels, gold, carriages, houses. But the little man tapped his foot impatiently.

"What do I want with all that stuff? You know I can turn even straw into gold. I want something alive."

But when he saw how distressed the queen was, he gave her one more chance.

"I'll give you three days to guess my name. If you can't, then the child is mine." Then he vanished. The next day he was back and the queen began, "Is your name Caspar? Melchior? Balthasar . . . ?" and she worked her way through all the names in the Bible. But, by the end of the day, the little man had said no to every one.

On the second day, she tried all the weird names she could think of, like Shortshanks and Grungefoot and Lumpybottom. The little man became more and more insulted, but the queen still hadn't discovered his real name.

That night she was in despair as she rocked her baby boy. She thought she would never guess the little man's name in time. Then she heard two of her servants talking. One had been out in the forest and had come to a hut with a fire outside it.

"And dancing round the fire was a funny little man singing a song," said the servant. "It went like this:

'Today I'll brew, tomorrow bake,
Then have the princeling, no mistake.
I need no fortune nor no fame,
RUMPELSTILTSKIN is my name!'"

The queen was so excited. Next day, when the little man came, she asked, "Is your name Leonardo?"

"No," said the little man.

"Is your name Brad?"

"No, no," said the little man. "You'll never get it!"

"Then," asked the queen, "is your name . . . Rumpelstiltskin?"

"Who told you, who told you?" screamed the little man, stamping his foot on the floor in such a rage that it went right through the floorboards. He pulled at his leg so hard that he split himself in half, and that was the end of Rumpelstiltskin.

The Three Billy Goats Gruff

Once upon a time there were three goat brothers who lived in a field together. They spent their days munching the long green grass and then skipping and playing around in their field.

But one day, they noticed that the grass in the field didn't look so green any more.

"Look," said Great Big Billy Goat Gruff. "We've eaten all the best grass. It seems much greener in that field there over the wooden bridge."

"That's right," said his brother, Middle Billy Goat Gruff. "That grass is much lusher and juicier than ours."

"So why don't we go there?" said their baby brother, Little Billy Goat Gruff.

"Mmm," said Great Big Billy Goat Gruff. "It's not as simple as that. You see, there's a bad old troll living under that bridge. He tries to eat everyone who crosses over."

"Then we must think of a plan," said Little Billy Goat Gruff.

Next morning, the bad old troll was sleeping under his bridge, when he heard the sound of hooves trit-trotting across the wooden planks.

"Goodie," he thought. "Here comes breakfast. I haven't had anything to eat for days."

And he started to sing a horrid little song:

"I'm a troll,

fol-de-rol,

I'm a troll,

fol-de-rol,

I'm a troll,

fol-de-rol—

And I'll eat you for my breakfast!"

And he leapt out from under the bridge to pounce on Little Billy Goat Gruff who was trit-trotting over the wooden bridge.

Little Billy Goat Gruff's heart was pounding, but he bravely stood his ground.

"Please, Mr Troll," he said, "I don't think that's a good idea. You see, I'm only a little kid and I wouldn't make much of a meal for you. In fact, I wouldn't be more than a mouthful. Why don't you wait for my big brother? He'll be along in a minute and he's much bigger than me."

The hairy troll scratched his head.

"Well, all right. If you're sure he's coming soon."

And he let the little kid trit-trot on over the bridge and into the new field.

The troll spent a very hungry morning until he heard the sound of some more hooves clip-clopping over the wooden bridge.

"Aha!" thought the troll. "That little kid was telling the truth. My tummy will soon be full."

And he started to sing his song again:

> "I'm a troll,
> fol-de-rol,
> I'm a troll,
> fol-de-rol,
> I'm a troll,
> fol-de-rol—
> And I'll eat you for my dinner!"

Out jumped the troll and there was Middle Billy Goat Gruff halfway across the bridge. He looked much meatier than his little brother.

"Oh, Mr Troll," said Middle Billy Goat Gruff. "You don't really want to eat me.

I'd only make a snack for a large troll like you. Why don't you wait for my big brother, who will be coming along soon?"

The troll was really hungry now, but he was also very greedy and he liked the idea of eating an even bigger goat. So he let the middle brother go clip-clopping on his way across the bridge and into the other field.

All afternoon the troll listened out for the sound of his goat meal trying to cross the bridge but all he could hear was the rumbling of his own tummy. And then, at last, when the sun was going down, the bridge started to tremble and the sound of hooves came stomp-stamping over the wooden bridge.

Aha! thought the troll and out he leapt, singing:

> "I'm a troll,
>   fol-de-rol,
>   I'm a troll,
>   fol-de-rol,
>   I'm a troll,
>   fol-de-rol—
>   And I'll eat you for my supper!"

When he saw Great Big Billy Goat Gruff, the troll's mouth began to water. The other goats had been right: there was plenty of eating on their big brother. But what was this?

The big goat wasn't frightened by the troll and his song. Great Big Billy Goat Gruff lowered his big head, with its big horns, and charged. He butted the troll high up into the sky . . .

Over the fields . . .

Over the hills . . .

. . . and right over the sun, till he was quite out of sight. And the bad old troll was never seen again.

Then Great Big Billy Goat Gruff stomp-stamped on his way, over the wooden bridge, and joined his brothers in the field where the grass was green as green. And for all we know, they are living there still.

The Hare
and the Tortoise

The hare and the tortoise were having an argument over who could travel faster.

"It's obviously me," said the hare, appealing to all the other animals who were listening. "I mean, look at the size of my back legs! And I'm famous for my leaping and bounding through the fields."

"True, true," agreed the badger and the fox and the field mouse, nodding their heads.

The tortoise shrugged.

"We shall see," he said. "If you're so sure, you won't mind having a race with me."

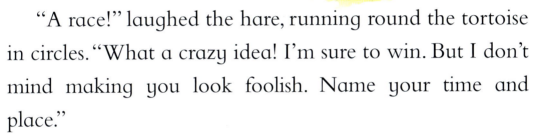

"A race!" laughed the hare, running round the tortoise in circles. "What a crazy idea! I'm sure to win. But I don't mind making you look foolish. Name your time and place."

The animals settled on a race from the big oak tree in the hedge to the elm at the corner of the field, to be held at sunrise the next day.

Next morning, the tortoise was at the oak tree bright and early and, as soon as the sun rose, he set off across the field at a steady pace.

The hare, on the other hand, overslept. When he saw that the sun was already climbing high in the sky, he thought, "It will take the tortoise ages to get from one tree to the other. There's still plenty of time for me to overtake him."

And he yawned and went back to sleep. Meanwhile, the tortoise was plodding his way determinedly along the race course at about a quarter of a mile an hour.

By the time the hare woke up and got himself to the oak tree, he could see the dark hump of the tortoise's shell moving through the corn near the elm.

"Help!" thought the hare, and he put on all the speed

he could with his big long back legs. But it was too late. As the hare reached the elm tree, panting with his efforts, the tortoise was already being congratulated by all the other animals on having won the race!

"But that's ridiculous!" gasped the hare. "Anyone can see I'm faster than he is!"

"Nevertheless," said the tortoise calmly, "slow and steady wins the race."

And there was nothing the hare could do about it except go back to his den and sulk.

The Three Sillies

There was once a farmer and his wife who had a very pretty daughter. But although she was pleasing to look at, she was not very clever—and this was not surprising, for her parents were not very clever either. But this foolish pretty girl was being courted by a gentleman, who came for supper at the farmhouse every evening.

It was the girl's job to go down to the cellar and draw a jug of beer from the barrel that was kept down there.

One evening, when she was doing this, her attention wandered and she noticed a mallet wedged in the rafters above her head.

"Oh, wouldn't it be terrible," said the girl to herself, "if I married and my husband and I had a son and he grew up and came down here to draw some beer and that mallet fell on his head and killed him?"

And she was so upset by this dreadful idea that she sat down on the floor and threw her apron over her head and began to howl. After a while she was missed upstairs and her mother came to look for her. She found the beer running out of the barrel all over the floor and her daughter in floods of tears.

"Why, whatever's the matter?" exclaimed the mother.

"Only think, Ma," sobbed the foolish girl. "Suppose I got married and we had a son and he grew up and came down here to draw beer. There's a horrid old mallet up there in the rafters and it might fall down on his head and kill him stone dead!"

As soon as the mother had heard this awful suggestion, she, too, sat down and threw her apron over her head

and began to cry just as loudly as her daughter.

"I can't think what has happened to the women," said the farmer. "They're taking an awfully long time to draw a jug of beer. I'd best go down and see what's keeping them."

And when he got down into the cellar, the farmer saw his wife and daughter sitting with their aprons over their heads and crying fit to bust, while the beer ran all over the floor.

"What on earth has happened?" he asked, in some alarm.

"Why, husband," wept his wife. "The most terrible thing. Look at that mallet stuck in the rafters! Suppose our daughter married her suitor and they had a son and he grew up and came down here to draw beer and that horrid mallet fell on his head and killed him!"

"That's awful!" said the farmer and he sat down beside them and burst into tears too at the thought of his grandson's fate. The gentleman had been left all alone upstairs and soon became anxious about what had happened to the family, so he went down into the cellar to find them.

Imagine his surprise at finding all three sitting on the floor, which was awash with beer, crying their eyes out! He

stepped quickly to the barrel and turned the tap off.

"Will someone please tell me what is going on?"

"Alas," said the farmer. "Do you see yonder mallet stuck in the rafters? Suppose you marry my daughter and the two of you have a son and he grows up and comes down here to draw beer and that mallet falls on his head and kills him? Isn't that cause enough for grief?"

The gentleman could hardly speak for laughing. He went over to the mallet and pulled it out of the rafters and set it on a shelf.

"Dry your eyes, all of you. You really are the three silliest people I have ever met! Now I am going on my travels and if I can find three people sillier than you,

I shall come back and marry your daughter."

With that, he left the three sillies crying just as hard, because the girl had lost her sweetheart. He hadn't travelled far before he saw an old woman trying to persuade her cow to climb a ladder.

"Why are you trying to get your cow up the ladder?" he asked.

"Why, I want her to eat the grass growing on the roof of my cottage," said the old woman. "It's a shame to waste it. And she'll be quite safe because when I've got her up, I'll tie this string round her neck and pass it down the chimney and fasten it round my waist."

"But wouldn't it be easier just to cut the grass and throw it down to the cow?" the gentleman couldn't help saying.

The old woman took no notice of this suggestion and the gentleman travelled on. But he heard a shriek behind him and turned to see that the cow had been hoisted onto the roof. It had slipped and fallen back down to the ground, yanking the old woman up the chimney!

The gentleman laughed so hard at the sight of the old woman on the roof all covered in soot shaking her fist at the cow, who was now munching the grass in her garden, that he nearly fell off his horse.

"Well, there is one person sillier than my sweetheart and her parents," he thought.

He travelled on and found an inn in which to rest. He had to share a room with another traveller, a very pleasant man, who was a good companion. But in the morning, this fellow-traveller did something very strange.

He hung his trousers on the doorknob, then went to the other side of the room and took a run at them, trying to jump into them! He did the same thing several times, till he was sweating with the effort, while the gentleman looked on in astonishment.

The man mopped his brow. "These trousers are the invention of the devil!" he panted. "It always takes at least an hour to get into them. However do you manage to get dressed so quickly?"

So the gentleman showed him the easy way to put on trousers, though he could hardly do so for laughing. As he went on his way the gentleman thought, "There is another person sillier than my sweetheart and her parents."

He travelled to a village where there was a crowd of people gathered round the pond, with rakes and brooms and sticks.

"What's up?" he asked one of them.

"Nay, rather ask what's down," said the villager, "for look—the moon's fallen into the pond and we can't get it out."

In vain did the gentleman point up at the sky to show them that the moon was still there and that what was in the pond was just a reflection. The villagers didn't want to know and sent him on his way with many insults.

"Why," thought the gentleman. "There are many more sillies in this world than my pretty sweetheart and her good parents."

And he rode back to the farm and asked the farmer's daughter to marry him straight away. Which she did, and if they are not happy still, it is not my business or yours.

The Frog Prince

Long, long ago, when wishing was useful, there lived a king with a very beautiful daughter. She was so used to everyone telling her that she was lovely as the day, that to be truthful, she had become rather vain and silly and inclined to think that everyone should do as she said.

By the castle was an old dark forest and, at the edge of it, in the castle grounds, was a tall, shady lime tree. Under the lime tree was a well of clear, cool water beside which the princess liked to sit, playing with her golden ball.

One day, she was sitting by the well tossing the ball up in the air and catching it, tossing it up and catching it,

tossing it up and . . . oh! dropping it down the deep, deep well! The princess sprang to the rim of the well and looked down, but it was no good. She couldn't even see the bottom, let alone her golden ball. How she wept and wailed!

"What's the matter, princess?" said a deep voice. "You cry so hard that even a stone would have pity on you."

The princess looked up and saw a large frog sticking his big ugly head out of the well.

"Alas," she said, through her tears. "I have dropped

my golden ball down the well and it is so deep that I shall never get it back."

"Don't say that," said the frog. "I could get your plaything for you, but I'd want something in return."

"Anything!" said the princess, clapping her hands and quite cheerful again. "My clothes, my jewels, why, even my little golden crown."

"Pah!" said the frog. "What good are such things to me? I can't wear your clothes or your jewels and a frog would look silly in a crown. What I want is for you to love me and let me be your companion. Will you let me eat off your golden plate and drink from your golden cup and sleep in your golden bed?"

"Yes, yes, of course," said the princess impatiently. "Anything you want. Only do hurry and fetch me my ball."

The frog disappeared into the water in a shower of bubbles and was back in a trice, carrying the ball in his wide mouth. He spat it out on the grass and the princess, delighted to have her plaything back, wiped it on her silk gown and skipped back to the castle to change her clothes.

And did she thank the frog? No. Did she remember her promise to him? No. The poor frog hopped wetly after her, crying, "Wait for me, wait for me!" while the princess never even looked back.

As she was sitting down to supper with the king her father, there came the strangest sound, of something creeping splish, splash, splish, splash, up the grand marble staircase. There was a knock at the dining-room door and a deep voice said, "Princess, princess, let me in!"

Startled, the princess opened the door, but shut it again quickly when she saw the lumpy, bumpy face of the frog looking up at her. She went back to her place with a racing heart and flushed face.

"Why, whatever is the matter, my dear?" asked the king. "Is there a giant outside the door?"

"No, Father, it is not a giant, but just a disgusting old frog."

"A frog, my dear? What does a frog want with you?"

"Today my golden ball fell in the well and the frog got it back for me. And . . . and he made me promise he could be my companion in return. But I didn't imagine he could leave the well. And now here the horrid thing is."

And she started to cry some very small crystal tears which just wet her long lashes and made her eyes look pretty. But, to her astonishment, her father gave her a very stern look.

"A promise is a promise," said the king. "No matter to whom you make it."

And he made the princess open the door and let the frog in. The frog hopped slowly up to the table, for he was tired after his long journey from the well.

"Lift me up beside you," he cried.

The princess shuddered, but her father was still watching her seriously, so she did as the frog asked.

Her lumpy, bumpy new companion pushed his mouth into her golden plate and dipped his long tongue into her cup. And, strangely, the princess lost all her appetite and ate and drank no more of her supper.

When the frog was full, he said to the princess, "I am very tired. Now take me to your bedroom and let us both lie in your golden bed."

At this, the princess began to cry in earnest, for she hated the idea of the cold wet frog in her clean and comfortable bed. But the king was angry with her. "The frog kept his side of the bargain," he said. "Now you must keep yours."

So the princess held the frog at arm's length, from the tips of her fingers, and carried him to her room, where she put him in a corner. Then she went to bed and cried herself to sleep.

She was woken by the clammy frog trying to climb into her bed.

"Lift me up!" he said, "or I shall tell your father."

So she did.

"Now, princess, if you are my loving companion, as you promised," said the frog, "you must kiss me goodnight."

How the princess screwed up her pretty eyes so that she might not see him and how she screwed up her pretty nose that she might not smell him and how she screwed up her pretty mouth that she might not taste him! And she gave the frog the quickest little peck of a kiss that she could get away with.

There was a rushing sound in the room and, when the princess opened her eyes, there was no frog to be seen.

Instead of his ugly, warty face, there gazed back at her the handsomest prince she had ever seen!

Immediately he went down on one knee.

"Thank you, thank you, beautiful princess," he said. "You have broken the spell. A witch changed me into a frog and condemned me to live in that cold dark well until a beautiful princess released me with a kiss."

Imagine the princess's confusion! But her father had told her she must be a loving companion to the frog. So the princess suddenly discovered she was very obedient and married her frog prince and lived happily ever after.

Cinderella

There was once a worthy man who was married to the best woman in the world. All her qualities of kindness, gentleness and beauty she left to her only daughter, Ella. That was the only legacy Ella had when her sweet mother died, for her father was short of money. He soon married again, and this time took a wealthy widow for his wife.

Ella's stepmother was as proud and vain as her real mother had been modest and unaffected. And, worst of all, she had two daughters of her own already, who took after her in their bad natures and cruel behaviour. As soon as generous soul that she offered to do their hair for them.

And when the great day came, as she was combing and curling and brushing and arranging their hair, one of the stepsisters asked her, "Wouldn't you like to come to the ball yourself?"

"Very much," replied Cinderella, "but I should look out of place among fine ladies like yourselves."

"Quite right," said the other stepsister. "Who would want to see a dirty cindery creature like you in a ballroom?"

It says a lot for Cinderella's sweet nature that she didn't pull their hair or make it stick up in ugly tufts, but carried on with her task bravely and in silence.

But when the carriage had taken her father and his new family to the ball, she sank onto a kitchen chair and sobbed. Then, all of a sudden, her fairy godmother appeared and said to Cinderella, "Why are you crying, child?"

Cinderella was too upset to be surprised. "Because . . . because I should so like . . ." But she couldn't finish.

" . . . to go to the ball?" guessed her godmother, and Cinderella nodded.

"Then go to the ball you shall," she said.

"But I have nothing but rags to wear!" said Cinderella. "And how should I get there? My father has taken the carriage."

"Have you forgotten I'm a fairy?" asked her godmother. "Now, there's no time to lose. Go into the garden and fetch me a pumpkin from the vegetable patch."

Cinderella didn't stop to ask why. She ran into the garden and cut the biggest pumpkin, that she had been saving to make soup with, and brought it back to her godmother. The fairy took it into the courtyard, scraped it out till just the rind was left, then tapped it with her wand.

And there before Cinderella's eyes was a handsome gilded coach, fit for a princess. "Now, go and see if there are any mice in the mousetrap," said the fairy.

Cinderella found six white mice, all alive, and the fairy tapped each one, turning it into a fine grey horse. So now there was a team of horses to pull the coach. Cinderella clapped her hands.

"What shall we do for a coachman, Godmother? I know—I'll look for a rat in the rat trap."

And she brought her godmother a rat, with long whiskers. One tap of the fairy's wand turned him into a coachman with a particularly fine moustache. "Go and fetch me the six lizards you will find behind the water-butt," said the fairy, and when

Cinderella had brought them to her, she turned them into six footmen in handsome shiny livery.

So now Cinderella had a very grand way of getting to the ball, but she was still standing in the courtyard in her rags.

"Now for you, my dear," said the fairy, and tapped Cinderella herself with the wand. In a trice, the poor ragged girl was transformed into a princess, wearing a ballgown of gold and silver, her hair dressed in a beautiful style and her throat circled by diamonds. To finish off her outfit was a dainty pair of glass slippers.

"You will be the belle of the ball, said her godmother, as she handed Cinderella into the coach. "But I must warn you that at midnight, everything will return to its usual shape and all your finery will disappear. You must be sure to leave the ball in good time."

"I will, Godmother," promised Cinderella. "And thank you for everything."

At the ball, the stepsisters were all of a flutter every time the prince danced past them. He was very good-looking and they both decided they would like him for a husband. While they were arguing about which of them he would ask to dance first, a beautiful and mysterious princess arrived in the ballroom.

No one knew who she was, perhaps a visitor from a foreign country? But the prince noticed her straight away and from then on had eyes for no one else. He danced with Cinderella all evening, although she would not tell him her name or anything about herself. She had the most wonderful evening of her life. Her beauty had charmed the king himself, who gave her special sweetmeats from his own plate, which she took great pleasure in sharing with

her stepsisters. They, of course, did not recognise her.

Then there were more dances with the prince and the hours just flew by. Before she knew it, Cinderella heard the clock beginning to strike twelve. "Oh, no!" she thought, and she ran out of the ballroom so fast that she didn't even say goodbye to the prince. As she ran down the stairs to her coach, she lost one of her glass slippers, but had no time to pick it up.

And, of course, by the time she reached her coach, there was nothing to be seen but a pumpkin and some garden animals, and her splendid clothes had turned back to rags.

Poor Cinderella had to walk barefoot all the way home (she put the remaining glass slipper in her pocket). She was cold and tired by the time she got there and, not long afterwards, her stepsisters arrived home and wanted to tell her all about the ball.

Cinderella didn't have to pretend that she hadn't been anywhere; she looked so pale and tattered, no one would have guessed she had danced with a prince at a grand ball. Certainly not her stepsisters.

"Oh, you should have seen the fine dresses and jewels!" they said, as Cinderella unhooked, unlaced and removed all their finery.

"And one guest in particular," they said, "was

astonishingly beautiful
and grand. She shared
the king's sweetmeats
with us."

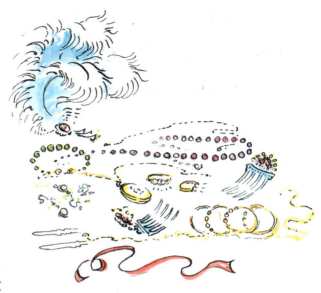

Cinderella couldn't
help smiling through her
yawns.

The next morning,
everyone was slow to get
up, which was just as well, for poor Cinderella overslept
too. But her stepmother and stepsisters were all cross.
Their tea was too cold, their toast too brown, their
butter wouldn't spread and their napkins weren't folded
properly.

But, in the middle of all their complaints, there came
a loud knock on the door. It was a messenger from the
prince. What a flutter that caused in the stepsisters' hearts!
It seemed that the prince was sick with love for the
mysterious princess and wanted to marry her. Since
she had left behind one of her glass slippers, he had
decreed that every young woman in the kingdom should
try it on. The prince would marry the one it fitted.
The messenger had been searching all night, but the

slipper had fitted no one.

The stepsisters nearly fell over themselves in their haste to try on the slipper. But it was no good. Their feet were so big, they couldn't squeeze in more than their toes. Just then, Cinderella stepped forward. "May I try it on?" she asked.

"The cheek of the girl!" fumed her stepmother, but the messenger looked at her pretty face and saw that, in spite of her rags, she might be the one.

"My orders are to let every young woman try it," he said.

So Cinderella slipped her foot into the little glass shoe. Imagine her stepsisters' surprise! And imagine their even greater surprise when she drew out the other slipper from her pocket and put that on, too!

At that moment, her fairy godmother appeared again and struck Cinderella with her wand, so that she was once more dressed in gorgeous clothes. Now the stepsisters recognised the grand "princess" of the night before.

She went back to the palace with the messenger and was reunited with the prince. Within a few days they were married and Cinderella, who had such a sweet nature and was so happy, found two courtiers of good family to marry her stepsisters. And it must be said that they were a great deal nicer when they were rich and married than they had been before. But Princess Ella was already as nice as she could be and so she always remained.